SUPER SANDCASTLE
Animal Habitats

What Lives in the Rain Forest?

Oona Gaarder-Juntti
Consulting Editor, Diane Craig, M.A./Reading Specialist

ABDO Publishing Company

Published by ABDO Publishing Company, 8000 West 78th Street, Edina, Minnesota 55439. Copyright © 2009 by Abdo Consulting Group, Inc. International copyrights reserved in all countries. No part of this book may be reproduced in any form without written permission from the publisher. Super SandCastle™ is a trademark and logo of ABDO Publishing Company.

Printed in the United States.

Credits
Editor: Liz Salzmann
Content Developer: Nancy Tuminelly
Cover and Interior Design and Production: Oona Gaarder-Juntti, Mighty Media
Illustration: Oona Gaarder-Juntti
Photo Credits: AbleStock, Creatas, Digital Vision, IT StockFree, ShutterStock

Library of Congress Cataloging-in-Publication Data

Gaarder-Juntti, Oona, 1979-

What lives in the rain forest? / Oona Gaarder-Juntti.

   p. cm. -- (Animal habitats)

ISBN 978-1-60453-177-0

  1. Rain forests--Juvenile literature. 2. Rain forest animals--Juvenile literature. I. Title.

QH86.G33 25008

591.734--dc22

                2008005479

Super SandCastle™ books are created by a team of professional educators, reading specialists, and content developers around five essential components— phonemic awareness, phonics, vocabulary, text comprehension, and fluency— to assist young readers as they develop reading skills and strategies and increase their general knowledge. All books are written, reviewed, and leveled for guided reading, early reading intervention, and Accelerated Reader® programs for use in shared, guided, and independent reading and writing activities to support a balanced approach to literacy instruction.

About SUPER SANDCASTLE™

Bigger Books for Emerging Readers
Grades K–4

Created for library, classroom, and at-home use, Super SandCastle™ books support and engage young readers as they develop and build literacy skills and will increase their general knowledge about the world around them. Super SandCastle™ books are part of SandCastle™, the leading PreK–3 imprint for emerging and beginning readers. Super SandCastle™ features a larger trim size for more reading fun.

Let Us Know

Super SandCastle™ would like to hear your stories about reading this book. What was your favorite page? Was there something hard that you needed help with? Share the ups and downs of learning to read. We want to hear from you! Send us an e-mail.

sandcastle@abdopublishing.com

Contact us for a complete list of SandCastle™, Super SandCastle™, and other nonfiction and fiction titles from ABDO Publishing Company.

www.abdopublishing.com • 8000 West 78th Street
Edina, MN 55439 • 800-800-1312 • 952-831-1632 fax

CHILDREN'S DEPARTMENT
WOODSON REGIONAL LIBRARY
9525 S. HALSTED ST. 60628

Tropical rain forests only cover a small part of the earth. But they are home to more than half of the animals in the world. Rain forests are warm and get a lot of rain.

Where are rain forests?

Tropical rain forests are found near the earth's equator. These rain forests are located in South America, Central America, Africa, Southeast Asia, and Australia.

7

8

Poison Dart Frog

Animal class: **Amphibian**
Location: **Central America and South America**

Poison dart frogs can be many colors including red, yellow, and blue. Their bright colors warn predators that they are poisonous.

Poison dart frogs have sticky toe pads that help them climb.

Red-Bellied Piranha

Animal class: Fish
Location: South America

Piranhas live in rain forest rivers and streams. They have sharp teeth and strong jaws. A school of piranhas will work together to hunt larger animals.

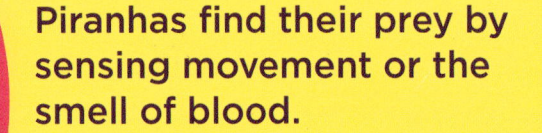

Piranhas find their prey by sensing movement or the smell of blood.

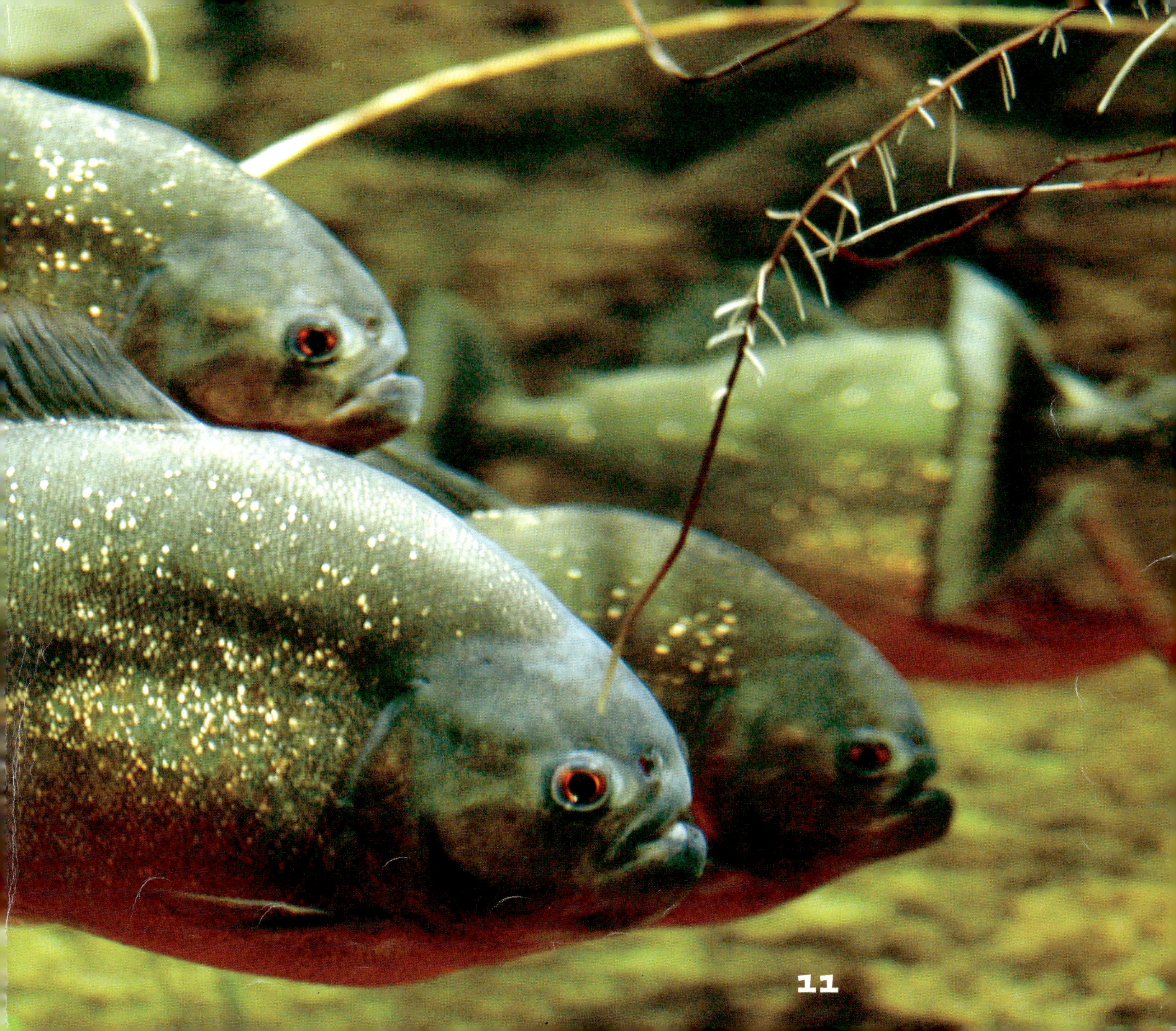

12

Green Tree Python

Animal class: Reptile
Location: Australia and Southeast Asia

The green tree python spends almost its entire life in the rain forest canopy. It will lie with its body coiled and draped over a branch. It often rests its head in the middle.

Female green tree pythons go to the forest floor to lay their eggs.

Keel-Billed Toucan

Animal class: Bird
Location: Mexico, Central America, and South America

Keel-billed toucans make their nests in tree holes. Several toucans often share a nest.

Toucans can't fly very well. They move from tree to tree by hopping.

15

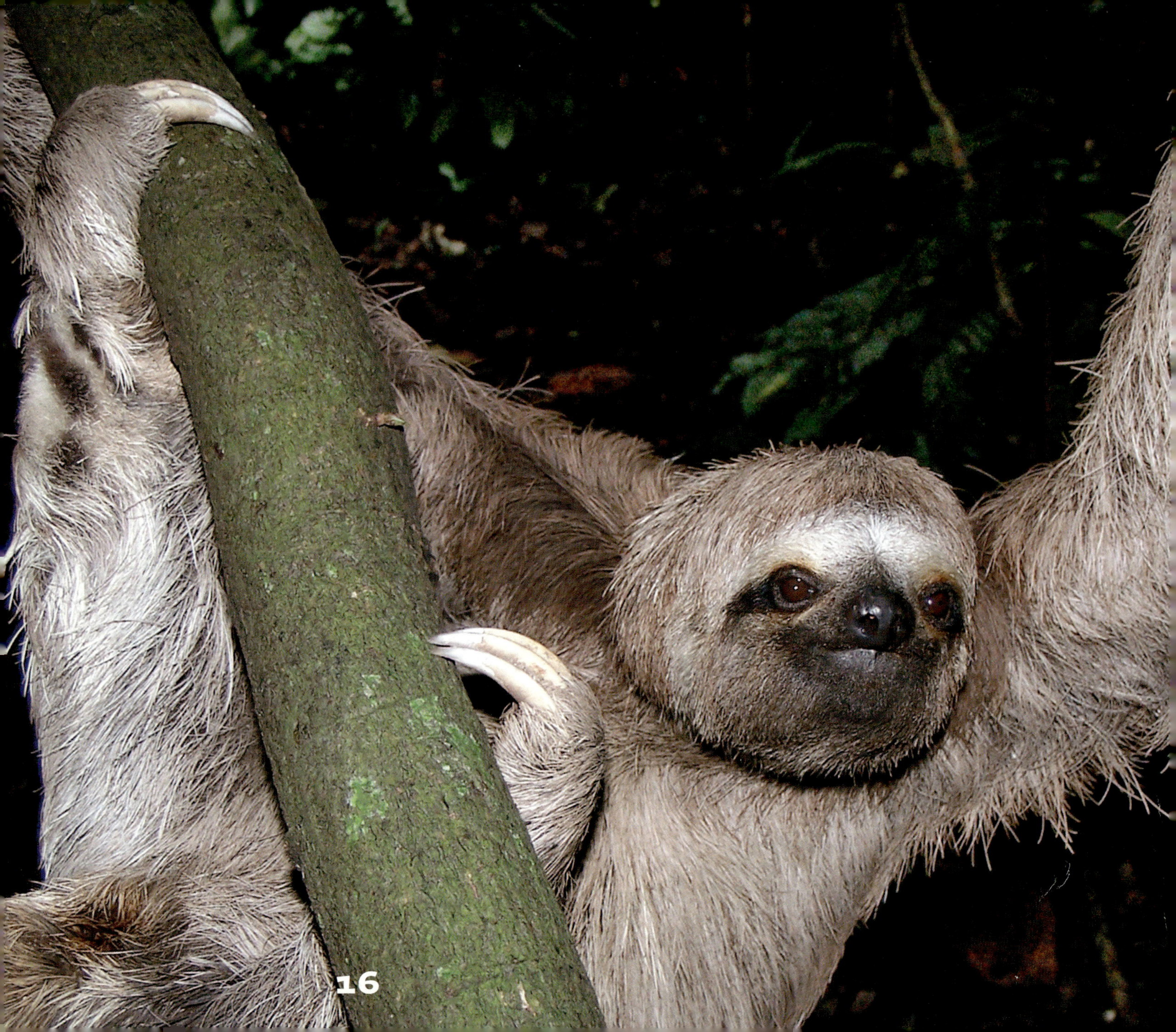

Three-Toed Sloth

Animal class: Mammal
Location: Central America and South America

Three-toed sloths have three curved claws on each foot. They hang upside down from tree branches. They sleep for 15 to 20 hours a day. Sloths move very slowly.

There are also two-toed sloths. They have two claws on their front feet and three claws on their back feet.

Okapi

Animal class: Mammal
Location: Central Africa

The okapi has stripes like a zebra but is related to the giraffe. It has a long blue tongue that it uses to grab leaves, grasses, fruits, and berries.

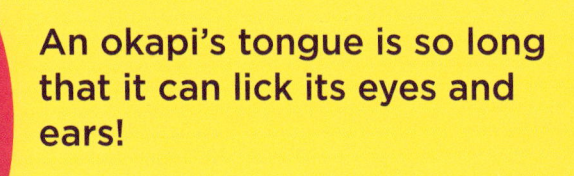

An okapi's tongue is so long that it can lick its eyes and ears!

19

20

Orangutan

Animal class: Mammal
Location: Islands in Southeast Asia

Orangutans spend most of their time in the canopy. They use their long arms to swing from branch to branch. Orangutans are the largest mammals that live in trees.

Orangutans stay with their parents until they are six or seven years old.

Have you ever been to a rain forest?

More Rain Forest Animals

Can you learn about these rain forest animals?

- anaconda
- caiman
- capybara
- chameleon
- chimpanzee
- duck-billed platypus
- great hornbill
- gorilla
- green-eyed tree frog
- howler monkey
- jaguar
- king cobra
- lemur
- macaw
- ocelot
- quetzal
- tapir
- tiger

Glossary

coil – to wind or twist into a ring or spiral shape.

drape – to hang loosely.

equator – an imaginary line around the earth that is an equal distance from the north and south poles.

female – being of the sex that can produce eggs or give birth. Mothers are female.

mammal – a warm-blooded animal that has hair, and whose females produce milk to feed the young.

pad – a soft, thick area on the bottom of an animal's toe or foot.

poisonous – containing a substance that can injure or kill.

predator – an animal that hunts others.

prey – an animal that is hunted or caught for food.

tropical – located in the hottest areas on earth.

vine – a plant that has a long stem that grows along the ground or clings to things such as trees.

wingspan – the distance from one wing tip to the other when the wings are fully spread.